Tyrannosaurus rex

Parasaurolophus

Stegosaurus

Diplodocus

Suchomimus

Compsognathus

Triceratops

Pachycephalosaurus

Pterodactyl

Plateosaurus

Ankylosaurus

Sinosauropteryx

Allosaurus

Velociraptor

Iguanodon

Archaeopteryx

Brontosaurus

Oviraptor

To Macey-Jayne,
sweet dreams always – M.S.

To KN for all his
support and
friendship – T.B.

Published in the UK by Scholastic, 2021
Euston House, 24 Eversholt Street, London, NW1 1DB
Scholastic Ireland, 89E Lagan Road, Dublin Industrial Estate,
Glasnevin, Dublin, D11 HP5F

SCHOLASTIC and associated logos are trademarks and/or
registered trademarks of Scholastic Inc.

Text © Mark Sperring, 2021
Illustrations © Tim Budgen, 2021

The rights of Mark Sperring and Tim Budgen to be identified
as the author and illustrator of this work have been asserted
by them under the Copyright, Designs and Patents Act 1988.

PB ISBN 978 0702 30423 1

A CIP catalogue record for this book is available from the British Library.

Printed by Printed by L.E.G.O. S.p.A, Italy
Paper made from wood grown in sustainable forests and other controlled sources.

3 5 7 9 10 8 6 4 2

This is a work of fiction. Names, characters, places incidents and
dialogues are products of the author's imagination or are
used fictitiously. Any resemblance to actual people,
living or dead, events or locales is entirely coincidental.

www.scholastic.co.uk

FSC
www.fsc.org
MIX
Paper from
responsible sources
FSC® C023419

MARK SPERRING   TIM BUDGEN

20 DINOSAURS at BEDTIME

■SCHOLASTIC

Once upon a bedtime,
these children
could not sleep,

ROAR!

so, their helpful mums
and daddies said
that they should
count some sheep.

Though children think
that sheep are nice,
there's something
they like more.

So, instead of counting
lots of sheep,
they counted . . .

Dinosaurs!

1...

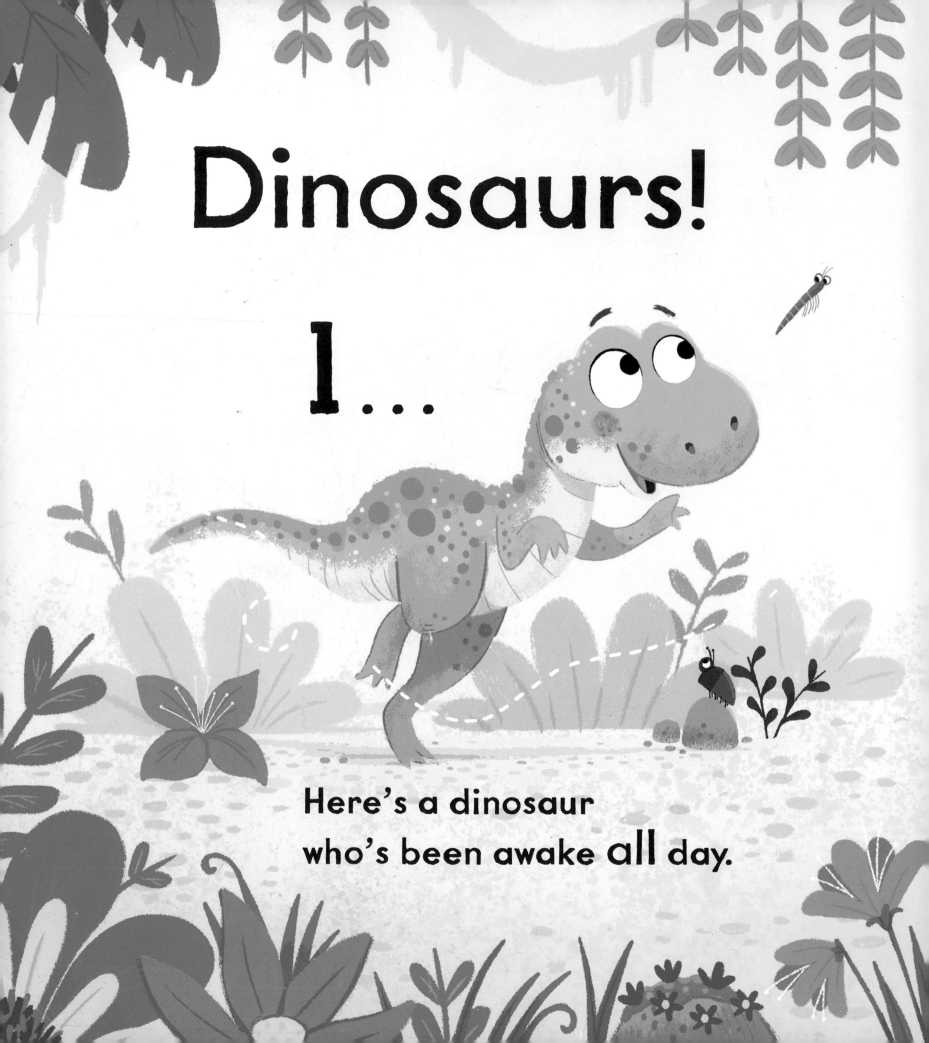

Here's a dinosaur
who's been awake all day.

2...

Here's a dinosaur
who wants to
roll and play.

3...

Here's a dinosaur
splashing
through the mud.

4...

Here's a
dinosaur
whose
giant feet go

THUD!

5...

Here's a dinosaur
chasing its own tail.

6...

Here's a dinosaur...

who's **slightly** scared of snails!

7...

Here's a dinosaur
watching the sun set.

8...

Here's a dinosaur

who isn't tired yet.

9...
Here's a dinosaur who's counting fireflies.

10...
Here's a dinosaur with very sleepy eyes.

11...
Here's a dinosaur
whose wings are
tucked up tight.

12...
Here's a dinosaur who's
whispering, "Goodnight!"

Yes, once upon a bedtime,

while counting
dinosaurs,

this bedtime-bunch snuggled down

and gave loud, sleepy snores.

But, in their dreams
they kept on counting
dinosaurs they met . . .
13 . . .

14 . . .

15...

And they've not stopped counting yet!

16...

Here's a dinosaur that
made a squeak then
hatched!

18...

Here's a dinosaur
in a leafy nest.

19...

Here's a dinosaur who
knows it's time to rest.

20!

Here's a dinosaur –
the last one that they found,

it gave them such a playful nudge,
then scooped them off the ground.

They walked through starlit forests
and bathed in the moon's soft light.

Once upon a bedtime,
on a count-to-twenty night!